Remembering Blue Fish

adapted by Becky Friedman
based on the screenplay "Daniel's Goldfish Dies" written by Becky Friedman
poses and layouts by Jason Fruchter

Simon Spotlight
New York   London   Toronto   Sydney   New Delhi

SIMON SPOTLIGHT
An imprint of Simon & Schuster Children's Publishing Division
1230 Avenue of the Americas, New York, New York 10020
This Simon Spotlight paperback edition August 2017
© 2017 The Fred Rogers Company
All rights reserved, including the right of reproduction in whole or in part in any form.
SIMON SPOTLIGHT and colophon are registered trademarks of Simon & Schuster, Inc.
For information about special discounts for bulk purchases, please contact Simon & Schuster
Special Sales at 1-866-506-1949 or business@simonandschuster.com.
Manufactured in the United States of America 0717 LAK
10 9 8 7 6 5 4 3 2 1
ISBN 978-1-5344-0095-5 (pbk)
ISBN 978-1-5344-0096-2 (eBook)

It was a beautiful day in the neighborhood, and Daniel Tiger and Baby Margaret were playing together.

"Blub, blub, blub. I'm a great big whale!" said Daniel.

"Blub blub blub," said Margaret.

Daniel chased Margaret around the living room.
"Look out, Margaret fish, Daniel the whale is coming to get you!"
"Blub blub blub," said Margaret as she ran away, giggling.

Daniel followed Margaret all the way over to the fish tank. He stopped and watched the fish.

Daniel saw his favorite fish, Blue Fish, near the little castle. "Hi, Blue Fish! You love your underwater castle, don't you?" said Daniel. "I wish I could swim in it with you."

Daniel imagined that he was swimming in the fish tank with all his fish.

Daniel watched the fish swimming around, but he noticed that Blue Fish wasn't swimming like the others. Blue Fish was lying at the bottom of the tank.

"Dad!" called Daniel. "I think something is wrong with Blue Fish!"

Dad Tiger walked over and looked at the fish with Daniel. "Blue Fish isn't moving. Is he sleeping?" asked Daniel. "I don't think so," Dad said gently. "I think Blue Fish is dead."

"Ask questions about what happened, it might help," sang Dad.

"What does it mean that Blue Fish is dead?" asked Daniel.

"It means that Blue Fish isn't breathing or swimming anymore," said Dad.

"Ask questions about what happened, it might help," Daniel sang.

"Can Blue Fish play later?" asked Daniel.

"No. When a pet dies, it can't play anymore," said Dad.

"Ask questions about what happened, it might help," sang Mom.

"I'm sad Blue Fish died," said Daniel. "How can I feel better?"

"Sometimes making a drawing of what you're sad about can help you feel better," suggested Mom.

Daniel took out his crayons to make a picture of Blue Fish. "This was Blue Fish," Daniel said as he drew. "He was a smiley fish, and he loved to swim." Daniel drew Blue Fish's tank and castle too, and then he added some wavy lines for water.

Margaret came over and gave Daniel a hug. Then she took out her toy fish. She still wanted to play.

"No, Margaret. I don't want to play right now," said Daniel. "I'm still sad."

But Margaret didn't understand. She took Daniel's picture and ran to the living room.

Mom Tiger stopped Margaret and gave Daniel his picture back.

"I'm mad," said Daniel. "I didn't want Margaret to take my picture, and I didn't want Blue Fish to die."

"I'm sorry, Daniel," said Mom Tiger. *"Ask questions about what happened, it might help."*

"Peek-a-boo!" said Margaret, covering her eyes.

Daniel giggled. "Mom, do you think it's okay to laugh or play with Margaret, even though Blue Fish died?"

"Yes," said Mom. "It's okay to be happy sometimes and sad sometimes."

Daniel smiled. "Okay, Margaret, let's play!"

Daniel and Margaret played hide-and-seek, laughing together, until . . . Daniel got a grr-ific idea.

Daniel picked up his picture of Blue Fish and brought it over to the fish tank.

"Hi, fishies," said Daniel, holding up his picture. "This is a picture of Blue Fish I made. He doesn't live in the fish tank anymore."

Daniel showed Dad a blue rock that he'd found outside.
"I want to put a blue rock in the fish tank, to remind me of Blue Fish," said Daniel.
Dad helped Daniel lower the blue rock into the tank.
"Now we can always remember our friend Blue Fish," said Daniel.

I'm glad you were with me for happy times and sad times. You can find someone to talk to when you feel sad too. Ugga Mugga!